Dracula

Bram Stoker

Retold by Rosie Dickins

Illustrated by Victor Tavares

Reading Consultant: Alison Kelly
Roehampton University

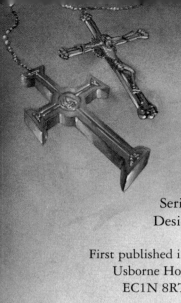

Series editor: Lesley Sims
Designed by Louise Flutter

First published in 2007 by Usborne Publishing Ltd.,
Usborne House, 83-85 Saffron Hill, London
EC1N 8RT, England. www.usborne.com

Printed in China. UE.
First published in America in 2008.

Contents

Chapter 1

Bad dreams

Jonathan ran. The wolf was close behind, a nightmare creature with blazing eyes and blood-stained fangs... it was almost on him...

Suddenly, he jolted awake. It took him a moment to remember where he really was — in a coach in Transylvania, on his way to see a wealthy count. The count wanted to buy a house in London and had hired Jonathan, a lawyer, to help him.

An eerie howl pierced the night. Jonathan shivered. "Get a grip," he told himself sternly. "It's just a dog... isn't it?"

The count had sent Jonathan directions.
They seemed simple enough...

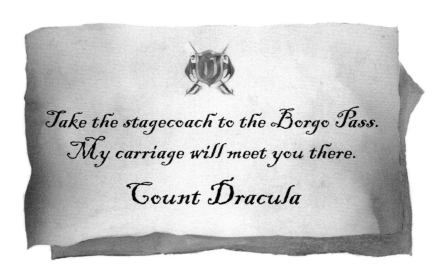

*Take the stagecoach to the Borgo Pass.
My carriage will meet you there.*

Count Dracula

But when the other passengers heard
where Jonathan was going, they gave him
sideways looks and muttered to each other.
Several times he thought he heard the
word *vampire.*

It was very late by the time they reached
the pass – only to find it deserted.

"I can't wait!" said the driver hastily. But before they could drive on, a black carriage with the count's coat of arms on it materialized out of the darkness. The driver crossed himself.

A chill swept over Jonathan. "If only I were at home with Mina!" he thought. But his beloved fiancée was hundreds of miles away.

Reluctantly, Jonathan got into the carriage and the mountains flew past.

Soon, he glimpsed a high castle, its broken battlements jagged against the sky.

The carriage stopped in a dark courtyard. A gaunt figure came to meet it, carrying a lantern. He smiled, revealing long, sharp teeth.

"Jonathan Harker? I am Count Dracula. Welcome to my castle."

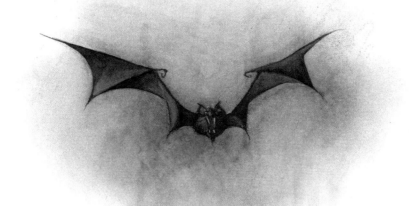

Chapter 2

Castle Dracula

The count held out his hand. When Jonathan shook it, it felt cold as ice.

"You must be hungry after your journey," said the count, leading him into a room where a delicious meal lay ready.

The count didn't touch a bite. "Tell me about the London house!" he demanded.

"It's called Carfax," Jonathan replied, between mouthfuls. "It's an ancient stone building with large grounds, surrounded by high walls..."

The next morning, Jonathan was
shaving when a sudden noise made him
jump. He spun around and nearly collided
with the count.

"I – I didn't see you in my mirror,"
stuttered Jonathan. The count didn't
seem to hear. He was staring intently at
Jonathan's chin. Jonathan put up his hand
and felt a trickle of blood.

"You should be more careful," hissed the count. "And I don't allow mirrors!" He flung Jonathan's shaving mirror out of the window and stalked away.

There was no sign of the count at breakfast, or after it. To pass the time, Jonathan decided to explore – but each door he tried was locked.

Eventually, he came to one door with broken hinges. He put his shoulder against it and shoved...

"Ugh!" He brushed a cobweb out of his eyes and looked around at a room full of heavy old furniture, covered in dust. The stale air began to make him feel sleepy. Yawning, he sank onto a couch.

As if in a dream, three women appeared.
They were very beautiful, with flashing eyes
and sharp, white teeth.

"Enough blood for us all," laughed one,
leaning over him.

Jonathan felt her teeth on his neck, but
he couldn't move. "Vampires," he thought
helplessly. "This is the end!"

Suddenly, he heard the count. "Stop! You
must not eat him – not *yet*." It was the last
thing Jonathan remembered...

When Jonathan woke, he was in his room. He sprang up and tried the door, but it was locked.

There were shouts under his window. In the yard below, some men were loading wooden boxes onto a cart.

"Help," he called. "I'm locked in. Can you help me?"

He thought the men nodded. But when they returned, it was with Dracula.

"You cannot leave," said the count bluntly. "I need you here."

"Yes, I'm sure you need me... so those women can eat me!" thought Jonathan. But he was too frightened to say anything.

Eventually, the men finished loading the boxes and the yard was deserted. Jonathan looked around carefully, then climbed out of his window...

To his dismay, the outer gates were locked. He looked around desperately. One door stood ajar – but the passageway beyond led only to a dark vault.

"Yuck!" He wrinkled his nose. The air smelled foul. Inside, someone had been digging up the ground. More wooden boxes lay around, half-filled with soil.

Jonathan stopped. There, in one box, lay Count Dracula, apparently asleep. His face was twisted in an evil smile and his lips were stained with blood.

"Help," gasped Jonathan. "He's a vampire too!" Filled with horror, he seized a shovel and swung it at Dracula... but his hand shook and he missed. The shovel struck the lid of the box and it slammed shut.

Terrified, Jonathan dropped the shovel and ran. "I've got to get out of here, even if I have to climb the walls!" he decided. "Oh Mina, will I ever see you again?"

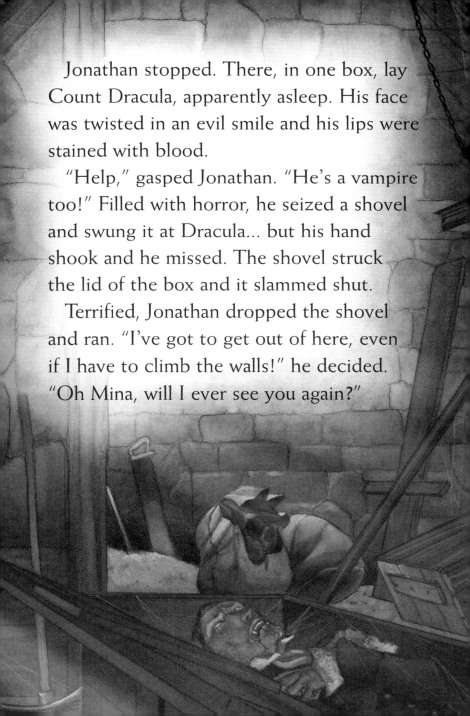

Chapter 3

A ghost ship

Jonathan, Jonathan... Mina stared out to sea, worrying about her fiancé. At her side, her friend Lucy was talking happily. Mina was staying with her for the summer. They were sitting on a bench outside the church on the cliff.

"I've been dying to tell you," Lucy giggled excitedly. "Arthur proposed – and I accepted!"

"Congratulations," said Mina. She couldn't keep the worry out of her voice.

"What's the matter?" asked Lucy.

"It's Jonathan," Mina admitted. "I haven't heard from him for weeks!"

Just then, it began to rain – heavy, stinging drops. Mina and Lucy had to run home. By the time they arrived, the rain was coming thick and fast and by nightfall, a fierce storm was raging. Lightning flashed and the wind whipped the sea into a fury.

"I hope there are no ships out there," whispered Mina, watching. Then a thick fog drifted in, as damp and clammy as ghosts' fingers, and the shore was hidden.

The next day, the storm was front-page news...

WORST STORM SINCE RECORDS BEGAN!

During the tempest, a mystery ship was driven ashore by the waves. Witnesses say there was no one on board except the captain – whose dead body was found lashed to the ship's wheel, clutching a crucifix.

OTHER NEWS

There have been several sightings of a huge dog or wolf near the coast...

Over lunch, Lucy's mother passed on the latest gossip about the ship. "Apparently, the ship's log told of a dark figure haunting the lower decks. One by one the crew disappeared, until only the captain was left..."

Lucy shivered. "He must have been terrified!" she said.

"And very brave, to get his ship safely to shore," added Mina. "Even if it meant dying at the wheel..."

Lucy's mother snorted. "It was hardly worth dying for that ship – all it was carrying was fifty boxes of soil!"

That night, Mina woke suddenly. She was sharing a room with Lucy, but the other bed was empty. She went to the window and saw Lucy in her nightdress, walking slowly, as if in a daze, in the direction of the cliff.

"Oh no," gasped Mina. "She must be sleepwalking." Mina grabbed a shawl and went after her friend. As she reached the clifftop, she saw Lucy lying on the bench – and a shadowy figure leaning over her.

"Lucy!" Mina called out, frightened.

Lucy didn't stir, but the figure looked up. There was a flash of red eyes, then it melted away into the darkness.

"I must be seeing things," muttered Mina, rubbing her eyes.

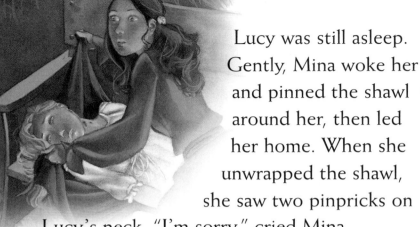

Lucy was still asleep. Gently, Mina woke her and pinned the shawl around her, then led her home. When she unwrapped the shawl, she saw two pinpricks on Lucy's neck. "I'm sorry," cried Mina. "I must have caught you with the pin."

All the next day, Lucy was tired and listless, and she insisted on going to bed early. Mina locked their door in case she tried to sleepwalk again.

She woke to find Lucy rattling the door handle, her eyes tight shut. Mina guided her back to bed.

A little while later, there was a scrabbling at the window. Lucy sat up in her sleep. Mina drew back the curtains and saw a giant bat flying away.

"How peculiar," she thought sleepily.

Mina meant to ask if anyone else had seen the bat, but the next morning, she had some news which made her forget all about it. There was a letter for her with an unfamiliar postmark.

"It's from a hospital in Budapest," she told Lucy, her voice trembling. "They say they're looking after Jonathan — something must have happened to him on his way home. He's been very ill. I must go to him at once!"

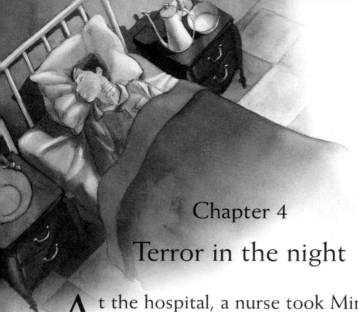

Chapter 4

Terror in the night

At the hospital, a nurse took Mina aside. "Your fiancé had a breakdown," she said. "He was found on a train, raving about blood and demons! Try to help him forget."

Mina gasped when she saw how haggard Jonathan looked.

"Oh Mina, I'm so glad you're here," he cried. "I can't tell you what I saw... I think I must have lost my mind!"

"My love," she whispered, wrapping her arms around him. "It's over now."

"Just concentrate on getting better, so we can be married. And speaking of marriage," she added, hoping to cheer him up, "I have some good news about Lucy and Arthur..."

But back at home, things weren't going well for the happy couple. Arthur was very worried.

"Lucy's so pale and tired all the time," he complained to their old friend Jack. "But she won't tell me what's wrong. She just says she's been having bad dreams. Jack, you're a doctor – will you talk to her?"

"Of course," promised Jack.

Arthur wasn't exaggerating. When Jack visited Lucy, she was very pale and weak.

Jack couldn't understand it. "I think there's something wrong with her blood," he confided to Arthur. "It's as though she doesn't have enough – but she hasn't been bleeding..."

"So what can we do?" interrupted Arthur impatiently.

"I'll send a telegram to my old teacher, Professor Van Helsing," replied Jack. "He's a blood specialist – he'll be able to help."

The professor arrived the very next day.
By now, Lucy looked ghastly. Her skin was
as white as chalk and she couldn't get out
of bed. The professor frowned.

"What is it?" demanded Jack.

The professor pointed to two small marks
on Lucy's neck, almost hidden by her hair.
"She needs an urgent transfusion," he cried.
"Arthur, we'll use your blood. Roll up your
sleeve..."

Arthur lovingly watched his blood flow
into his fiancée. "I've never felt closer to
anyone," he whispered. Already, the pink
was returning to Lucy's cheeks.

Next, the professor shut the window
and pulled out a bunch of white flowers.
A strong smell filled the air. He tucked
some flowers around the window frame,
then made the rest into a garland which
he draped around Lucy's neck. She smiled
peacefully and fell asleep.

Later that day, Lucy's mother bustled
in. "Ugh, garlic!" she sniffed, opening the
window and throwing out the flowers.

In the morning, the men returned to check on Lucy's progress. To their shock, she was worse — even her lips were white.

The professor scowled when he noticed the missing flowers. As soon as they had given Lucy another transfusion, he shut the window and brought in more blooms.

"But they smell terrible," protested Lucy's mother.

"The smell is part of the cure," the professor told her gravely. "To remove them would be dangerous... more dangerous than you know," he added under his breath.

That night, Lucy felt afraid to go to sleep. She heard something flapping at her window and sat up to see what it was.

"Just a bat," she told herself, watching it fly away.

"Are you all right, dear?" asked her mother, looking in. "I heard you moving around and..."

Outside, there was a piercing howl. Then something crashed against the window, shattering the glass... it was a huge wolf.

Lucy's mother made a choking noise. She clutched desperately at her daughter, then collapsed. Her heart, never strong, couldn't stand the shock. As she fell, her fingers caught Lucy's garland. The flowers broke and scattered across the floor.

A swirl of mist blew in through the broken glass and began to take shape...

Lucy screamed.

Chapter 5

Tragedy strikes

In the morning, Arthur, Jack and the professor returned to the house. To their surprise, the windows were all dark. However loudly they knocked, no one came.

"Something's wrong!" cried Arthur. He pushed desperately at the door until the lock snapped. The three men rushed straight to Lucy's room.

A terrible sight met their eyes. Lucy's mother lay dead on the floor and Lucy was sprawled across the bed, scarcely breathing.

The professor gently drew a sheet over the mother. Jack felt for Lucy's pulse. Her arm was as cold and white as marble.

"We must warm her up," he cried.

Arthur grabbed a blanket and wrapped it around her, and Jack lit a fire in the grate. Then they placed Lucy in a chair by the fire and rubbed her hands and feet.

The professor produced a small flask. "Brandy," he informed them, dribbling a little into her mouth.

Suddenly, Lucy sat up with a strange expression. Her eyes seemed hard and her lips were drawn back, showing her teeth.

She held out her arms to Arthur. "Kiss me, my love," she asked in a husky, unfamiliar voice.

"No!" shouted the professor, pulling Arthur back.

Lucy slumped and the glare went out of her eyes. "Thank you, professor," she said in her own voice a moment later. "You are a true friend."

"Now you may kiss her," said the professor, letting go of Arthur's arm.

Arthur took Lucy's hand and gently kissed her forehead.

Lucy smiled at him, then closed her
eyes for the last time. She looked as if she
had fallen asleep – but she was no longer
breathing.

"It's the end," sighed Jack.

"No," muttered the professor. "I'm
afraid this is only the beginning."

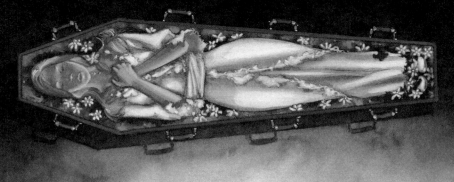

Chapter 6

The haunted graveyard

A joint funeral for Lucy and her mother was held a few days later. Arthur, Jack and the professor were all there. Mina and Jonathan – who had just arrived back from Budapest, newly married – came too.

Death seemed to have restored all of Lucy's youthful beauty.

"You'd hardly even know she was dead," gulped Arthur.

The professor frowned.

When the funeral service was over, the professor addressed the others. "There is something you must know," he began.

"Lucy did not die of natural causes. She was killed by a vampire... a monster which steals life by drinking the blood of others!"

"So they DO exist," gasped Jonathan. "I thought I'd lost my mind!" At last, he confessed what had really happened in Count Dracula's castle... "And now Dracula has moved to Carfax in London," he finished.

"We must stop this evil from spreading!" cried the professor.

Mina took her husband's arm. "We'll help," she said boldly. "What can we do?"

"First, we must deal with Lucy," said the professor. "Now she is dead, she too will become a vampire..."

"No," interrupted Jack. "It's impossible."

"And an insult to Lucy's memory!" added Arthur angrily.

"I can prove it," promised the professor. "Come with me to the graveyard tonight, you two, and you'll see for yourselves."

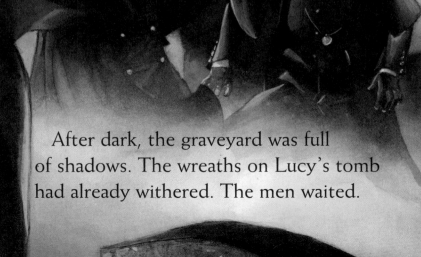

After dark, the graveyard was full of shadows. The wreaths on Lucy's tomb had already withered. The men waited.

Shortly before dawn a familiar figure appeared, dragging a young boy. Her eyes flamed and there was blood on her dress. When she saw Arthur, she let the boy go and held out her arms.

"Come, love, I am hungry for you," she whispered huskily.

"No," gasped Arthur, horrified. "That's not Lucy. It can't be..."

The creature laughed, revealing long, pointed teeth, and melted into the tomb.

"No, it's not Lucy," the professor said gently. "It is the vampire who has taken over her body. Killing it will free Lucy's soul. That will be an act of love — so you, Arthur, should be the one to do it."

Arthur's jaw set. "For Lucy," he said resolutely.

In the clear light of dawn, they opened the tomb. Inside, the vampire lay sleeping. Silently, the professor handed Arthur a sharpened stake, and he plunged it deep into the creature's heart. There was a blood-curdling screech... then silence.

When they looked again, Lucy's face wore its old expression of sweetness and purity.

"She is at peace," said the professor. "But our work is not done. Now we must find and kill Count Dracula, who is the source of this evil."

"I'm sorry I doubted you," said Arthur gruffly. "I'll do everything I can to help."

"So will I," promised Jack.

Chapter 7

A new victim

In Jack's house in London, the friends gathered to discuss their task.

"In his time, Dracula was a great warrior," said the professor. "Now, as a vampire, he is even stronger — as strong as twenty men. He can control the weather, and he can turn himself into a bat or a wolf. But his powers are limited to the hours of darkness. By day, he must rest in his ancestral soil. He cannot bear garlic, or holy water, or the sign of the cross. And he can be killed with a stake through the heart!"

"Dracula will have brought some of his accursed soil with him, to make a new lair," the professor continued.

"The ghost ship," breathed Mina. She told the others about the storm and the ship carrying fifty boxes of soil.

"We can sterilize the soil with holy water," said the professor. "We must leave this monster no place to hide!"

"Well, what are we waiting for?" asked Arthur impatiently. "Let's get into Carfax."

The Carfax house was a gloomy, derelict place. The friends had no trouble forcing their way in. Inside, it was thick with dust and a foul stench filled the air.

Dracula was nowhere to be seen, but boxes of soil were lying on the floor.

"Only twenty nine," muttered Jack, after a quick count.

"It's a start," replied the professor. They set about sprinkling the boxes with holy water. As they worked, rats began to pour out of the walls. Soon, the whole floor was alive with squirming rats.

"Let's get out of here," said Jonathan, hurriedly sprinkling the last box.

It was so late by the time they got home, they went straight to bed. Even so, Mina looked pale and tired in the morning. She admitted to sleeping badly.

"I remember a strange mist," she said. "Only I must have been dreaming, because it seemed to have red eyes..."

The professor spluttered into his tea.

The friends spent all day trying to trace the remaining boxes. That night, the professor waited for the others to go to bed. Then, clutching a crucifix, he burst into Mina's room. As he had feared, she was not alone. A dark figure with red eyes was hovering over the bed, while her husband sprawled unconscious on the floor.

"Dracula!" cried the professor, holding up his crucifix. The count snarled and backed away. A black cloud drifted across the moon and, for a moment, all was dark. When it passed, the count was gone.

Jonathan staggered to his feet. "Where's that monster?" he cried. "Let me at him!"

Mina clung to his arm. "It's too late," she sobbed. "That... that *thing* drank my blood – and then he made me drink his. He said he would make me a vampire, like him..." She broke off. Jonathan hugged her, unable to speak.

"Take this," said the professor softly, holding out his crucifix. But when it touched her, it burned her skin, leaving a cross-shaped scar.

Mina recoiled in horror. "What have I become?" she wailed. Then she took a deep breath and looked Jonathan in the eye. "You must promise me something."

Jonathan nodded mutely.

"If I start to change, if I become a threat... you must kill me."

"Mina, you are very brave," said the professor admiringly. "But that won't be necessary. We will defeat Dracula... I hope," he added, under his breath.

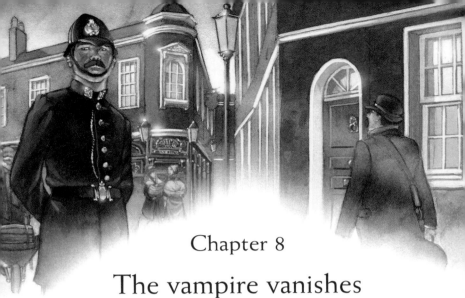

Chapter 8

The vampire vanishes

Breakfast was a miserable affair, but the
friends had one piece of luck. A letter
arrived for Jonathan, saying Dracula had
had some boxes delivered to an address
in Piccadilly. The men set off at once. It
turned out to be a house on a busy street,
with a policeman at the corner.

"We can't break in," said Jonathan.
"Everyone will see."

"Oh can't we?" replied Arthur. He
disappeared into a shop.

A few minutes later, he was back with a locksmith. "Thank you so much," he was saying. "I can't think how I lost my keys..."

Inside, the men were greeted by the same vile smell. The house was deserted, but there were boxes stacked in the hall.

"Only twenty," moaned Jonathan, as they sprinkled holy water. "One's missing."

Just then, they heard footsteps outside. The men glanced at each other and grasped their crucifixes tightly. A key rasped in the lock...

The door swung open and Dracula hurried inside – and froze. Jonathan lunged at him with a knife. Dracula dodged with inhuman speed, but the blade slashed his coat pocket and gold coins rained down. The count's eyes burned. He seized a fistful of coins and ran to the window, then turned like a creature at bay.

"You'll be sorry later, all of you," he snarled. "My revenge has just begun – and time is on my side!" With that, he smashed through the glass and vanished.

The men returned home downcast.

"He slipped right through our fingers," Jonathan told Mina angrily. "But I'll find him and finish him. And I hope his soul burns for all eternity!"

"The monster must be destroyed," said Mina gently. "But have pity on his soul. Remember, I may need your pity too..."

Jonathan clasped her hand very tightly.

Just before dawn, the professor heard a knock at his door. It was Mina and Jonathan. "Will you hypnotize me?" Mina burst out. "I can feel that creature in my thoughts and I want to free my mind..."

Startled, the professor asked Mina to sit down. He passed his hands across her face until her eyes closed. Then she spoke. "I am on a ship. It is dark, but I can hear the waves. I lie still... as still as death..."

"Astonishing," muttered the professor. "Her mind is linked to Dracula – she's describing him! And he's leaving. I think he's running away."

"Our job is done," said Jonathan.

"Far from it," sighed the professor. "Dracula cursed Mina. We must kill him, or she will become a vampire too."

Chapter 9

A deadly chase

Tracing Dracula proved easier than the friends feared. Only one ship had set sail for Transylvania the previous day – and its cargo list included a box of soil. "Its first port of call is Varna, on the Black Sea. We can get there faster by train," said Mina.

"You're not coming," objected Jonathan. "It's too dangerous."

"It's more dangerous if I stay," insisted Mina. "Already, my teeth are sharper. I'm changing, Jonathan! I dare not be alone."

The train journey took three days. The ship was meant to take three weeks. But the weeks passed and there was no sign of it. "Something's wrong," said Arthur. "I'm going to make inquiries." Next morning, he received a telegram:

To: Arthur Holmwood

Ship diverted
to Galatz.

"Dracula's avoiding us!" exclaimed the professor. "When I hypnotized Mina, the mind-reading must have worked both ways. We must leave at once."

At Galatz, the friends found the ship's captain. "A strange journey," he told them. "We were making good time until we were blown off course by a terrible storm...

And the fog! Most of the time we were sailing blind. The crew blamed it all on a wooden box we were carrying. They said it was haunted!"

"What happened to the box?" asked the professor anxiously.

"Some men collected it yesterday," said the captain. "And good riddance, too. I think they were taking it to the river."

"Look at the map," said Mina. "The river goes all the way to the Borgo Pass..."

"Let's split up," said Arthur. "Jonathan, Jack — we'll follow the river. If he's on a boat, we should be able to catch him. Professor, you take Mina and head for the castle, to deal with his lair."

"No!" exclaimed Jonathan, shuddering. "You don't know what that place is like — full of moonlight and monsters. You can't go there."

"There is no choice," said Mina, slowly. "We... must hurry..."

Jonathan looked closely at his wife. She was very pale and spoke with effort.

"She is fighting the change," whispered the professor. "But it's getting harder."

Jonathan bowed his head. "So be it," he said. "Heaven help us all."

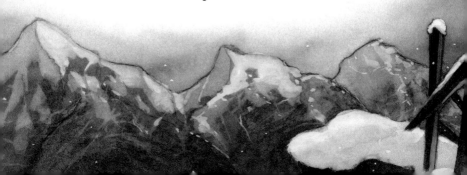

As soon as the friends had equipped themselves, they set off. Jonathan, Jack and Arthur rode off along the riverbank, their packs loaded with weapons. Mina and the professor hired a carriage.

The carriage sped over the roads and by nightfall, Mina and the professor were deep among the snowy mountains. When they stopped for the night, the professor pulled out a flask. "Holy water," he said. Before they went to sleep, he sprinkled a large circle around them.

As the moon rose, three women appeared out of the whirling snow. The carriage horses whinnied in terror.

"Vampires," muttered the professor.

The women drew closer, holding out their arms. "Come to us!" they called. But when they reached the edge of the circle, they stopped, baffled.

"Be gone!" cried the professor, brandishing his crucifix. They snarled and drew back. Then, as the sun climbed over the horizon, they melted away.

Mina and the professor reached the castle the next day.

By now, Mina was paler than ever. The professor left her in the carriage while he went to find the vault. Inside, there were four tombs. The largest was empty. It bore one word: Dracula.

In the other tombs lay three women. They looked so beautiful that the professor hesitated... "For Mina," he told himself. He plunged a stake deep into each vampire's heart. They screeched and writhed, and fell still. A look of peace stole over their faces. A moment later, they crumbled to dust.

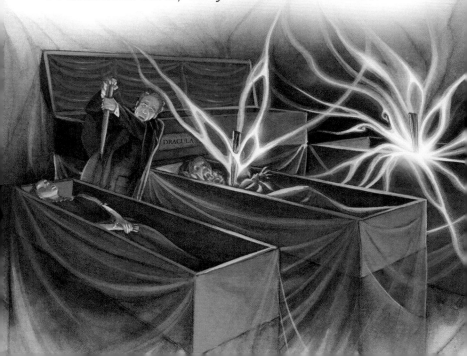

Before leaving, the professor sprinkled the whole place with holy water. By the time he got back to the carriage, the sun was low in the sky.

In the distance, wolves howled. Then he and Mina heard hoofbeats. They ran to the edge of the cliff and looked down.

Far below, there was a wagon carrying a box, lurching toward the castle at a crazy speed. Close behind rode Jonathan, Arthur and Jack, their guns at the ready.

As they watched, the friends caught up with the wagon and forced it to stop. The men on the wagon pulled out knives and formed a defensive circle. Their leader pointed at the setting sun and laughed. In answer, Jonathan, Arthur and Jack threw themselves forward.

Knives flashed and blows fell. Jonathan fought most furiously of all. His enemies fell away before him and moments later, he was beside the box.

Jonathan wrenched off the lid. Inside, scattered with soil, lay the count. He was deathly pale and his red eyes glared. As he caught sight of the setting sun, his lips twisted in a triumphant grin...

At that very moment, Jonathan's arm swept down, plunging a stake deep into the vampire's heart. Mina thought she saw a look of surprise – and then peace – steal over Dracula's face. A moment later, his body crumbled into dust.

The men on the wagon turned and fled.

Mina gave a cry and scrambled down the cliff to her husband. As Jonathan gathered her in his arms, he saw the cross-shaped scar had gone, leaving her skin as smooth and pure as new-fallen snow. "The curse is broken," he whispered.

Arthur rubbed his eyes. The professor put a hand on his shoulder. "I know you're thinking of Lucy," he said gently. "If only we could have saved her too... But we have rid the world of an ancient evil – and now her soul can truly rest in peace."

Bram Stoker (1847-1912)

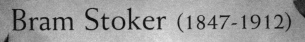

Bram Stoker was born in Ireland in 1847. As well as writing, he worked as a lawyer, a civil servant and a theatrical manager. He produced several books, but only *Dracula* is famous today.

In 1890, Stoker visited the English seaside town of Whitby. There, he began making notes for a story based on ancient vampire legends. Parts of Whitby also found their way into the story, including the church on the cliff where Mina and Lucy sit and talk.

Dracula was eventually published seven years later – and has never been out of print since. It has been translated into nearly fifty languages and has inspired countless films.

Stoker's story also helped popularize certain ideas about vampires – for example, that they are afraid of garlic and holy water. He also suggests that when a vampire is staked through the heart, its body returns to its natural state, so the most ancient vampires simply crumble into dust.